Mr Biff
the Boxer

by ALLAN AHLBERG

with pictures by
JANET AHLBERG

Puffin

Viking

PUFFIN/VIKING

Published by the Penguin Group
Penguin Books Ltd, 27 Wrights Lane, London W8 5TZ, England
Penguin Books USA Inc., 375 Hudson Street, New York, New York 10014, USA
Penguin Books Australia Ltd, Ringwood, Victoria, Australia
Penguin Books Canada Ltd, 10 Alcorn Avenue, Toronto, Ontario, Canada M4V 3B2
Penguin Books (NZ) Ltd, 182–190 Wairau Road, Auckland 10, New Zealand

Penguin Books Ltd, Registered Offices: Harmondsworth, Middlesex, England

First published 1980
17 19 20 18

Text copyright © Allan Ahlberg, 1980
Illustrations copyright © Janet Ahlberg, 1980

Educational Advisory Editor: Brian Thompson

Printed in Singapore by Imago Publishing Limited
Set in Century Schoolbook by Filmtype Services Limited, Scarborough

ISBN Paperback 0 14 03.1236 6
ISBN Hardback 0–670–80574–2

There was once a man named Mr Bop.
Mr Bop was a boxer.
He was as fit as a fiddle.
He was the toughest man in the town.
He was the champion.
There was another boxer in the town.
His name was Mr Biff.

Mr Biff was not as fit as a fiddle.
He ate too many cream cakes.
He drank too many bottles of beer.
Mr Biff was not tough.
He liked to sit in an easy chair
by a cosy fire.
He liked to put his slippers on
and read the paper.
He slept in a feather bed.

One day posters appeared in
the town. They said:

BIG CHARITY FIGHT
MR BIFF AGAINST MR BOP

Mr Biff told his wife
about the fight.
"It's for charity," he said.
"Me against Mr Bop."
"Oh dear," said Mrs Biff.
"They say he is the toughest man
in the town."
"They say his wife is the toughest
woman, too," said Mr Biff.

Mrs Biff told the children
about the fight.
"It's for charity," she said.
"Your dad against Mr Bop."
"Our dad will win," said Billy Biff.
"He will biff him!" Betty Biff said.

"But your dad is not fit,"
said Mrs Biff. "And he is not tough."
"We will be his trainers then,"
said Billy Biff.
"And toughen him up," Betty Biff said.
"You wait and see!"

The next day Mr Biff began training.
His family helped.
Billy Biff took him running.
Betty Biff took him skipping.

Mrs Biff hid his paper
and his slippers.
Bonzo Biff kept him out of
the easy chair.

The children also helped
to toughen him up.

Mrs Biff helped
to toughen him up too.

Mr Biff was put on a diet.
"I'd like three cream cakes
and a bottle of beer," he said.
"You can have three carrots
and a glass of water,"
said Mrs Biff.

Each day the children said,
"How do you feel, dad?"
Each day Mr Biff said,
"I feel terrible!"

But one day the children said,
"How do you feel, dad?"
And Mr Biff said,
"I feel as fit as a fiddle!"

Now it was the day of the fight.
A big tent was put up in the town.
Everybody was excited.
Crowds gathered.

The referee stepped into the ring.
"My lords, ladies and gentlemen,"
he said.
"On my right – Mr Bop!"
Everybody cheered.
"That's my husband!" said Mrs Bop.
"On my left – Mr Biff!"
Everybody cheered again.
"That's my dad!" Billy Biff shouted.

The time-keeper rang his bell.
"Ding-ding!"
The fight began.

Mr Biff stepped forward.

Mr Bop stepped forward

Mr Bop moved to the right.

Mr Biff moved to the left.

Suddenly Mr Bop bopped Mr Biff.
At the same time Mr Biff biffed
Mr Bop.
They biffed and bopped each other out!

"It's a draw!" the referee said.
The time-keeper rang his bell.
"Ding-ding!"
The fight was ended.

In the dressing-room Mr Biff said,
"How do you feel?"
"I feel terrible!" said Mr Bop.
"I think bopping people is silly."
"Biffing people is silly too,"
said Mr Biff.
Then Mr Bop said,
"I feel hungry as well.
I have been on a diet."
"Me too," said Mr Biff.

"I could just eat a cream cake now!"
"And a jam tart!" said Mr Bop.
"And fish and chips!" said Mr Biff.
"And roast chicken and potatoes
and peas, and bread and butter,
and a bottle of beer!" Mr Bop said.

So that evening the two families
went out for a big dinner.
Mrs Biff made friends with Mrs Bop.
The Biff children made friends
with the Bop children.

Bonzo Biff shared a bone with
the Bop dog.
And a happy time was had by all.

The End